THE BROWN CRAYON

Written by
Michael G. Williams

Cover illustration by
Laura Burress

This book is dedicated to the memory of
Clarence & Jannie Marie Williams.
Two people who loved me unconditionally and
taught me how to love everyone else the same
way!

Thank you Mom & Dad!

To my brother, Clarence, you taught me how
to lose, survive, start over, and win!

To GOD be the Glory!

Our teacher gave us a chance to pick a crayon from the bag. I looked around and saw all the pretty colors everyone had.

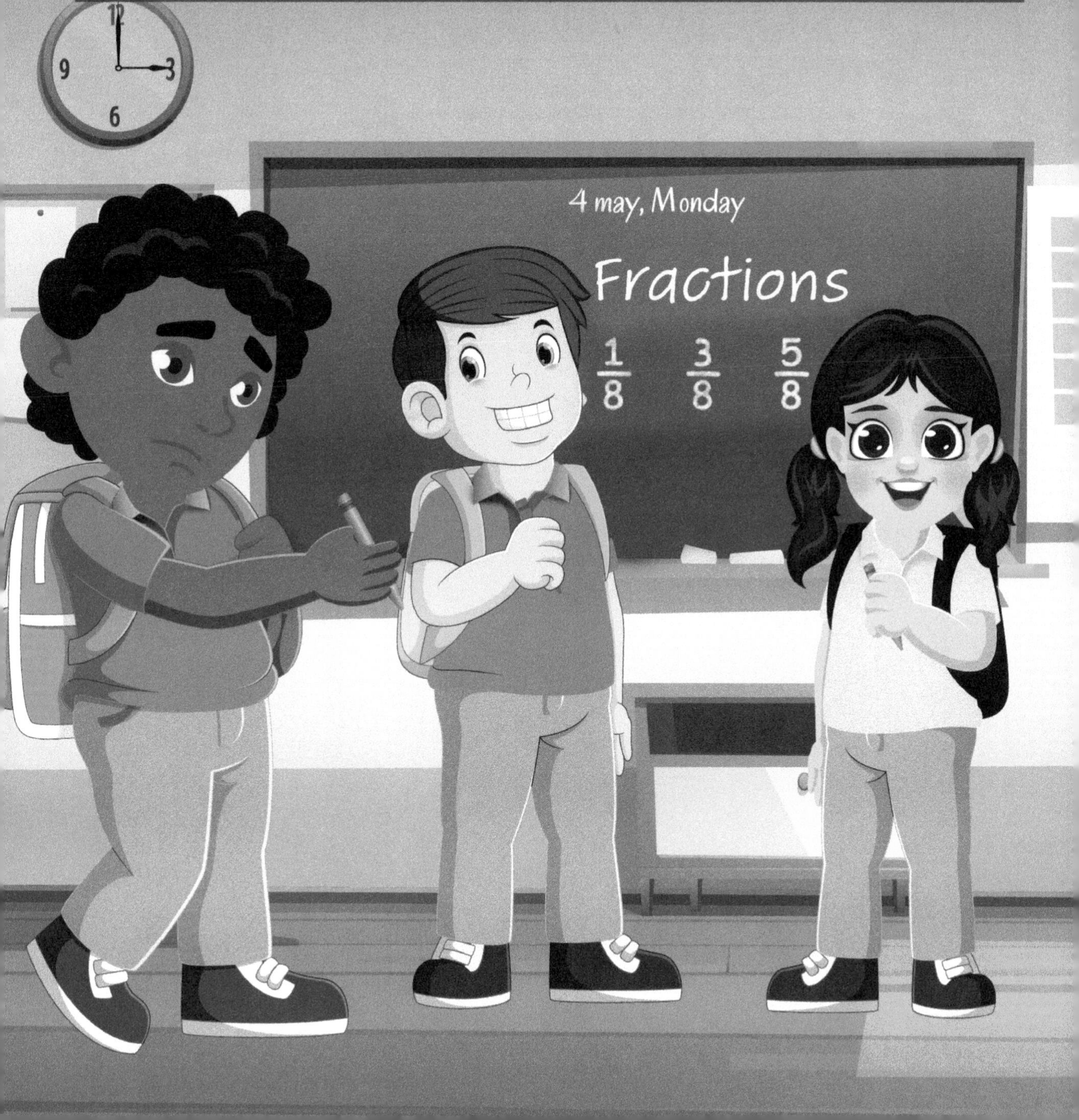

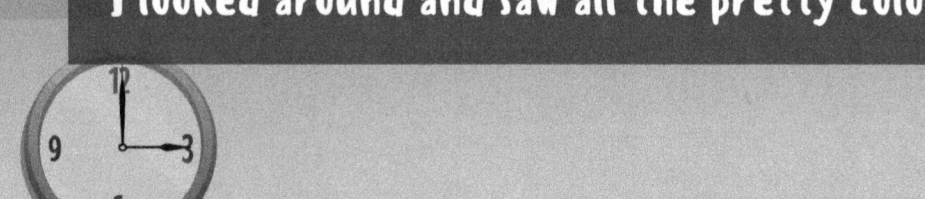

As I got in the car to go home with my parents, I looked next to me and smiling as always, was my little brother Clarence.

He doesn't know the tragic homework I have to write down. You see, I have to write a poem on the wonderful things about the color brown.

Well, dinner was over, dad was asleep with the TV watching him.
Mom was changing clarence and I was feeling pretty grim.

Grim like the color brown, that crayon begin to stare at me, and Booo! "I know," I said to the crayon, "I only got an hour to write why anybody should like you!"

So, with a bad attitude, I grab some paper and scooted up to the table. This has to be quick, I've got to get back to cable!

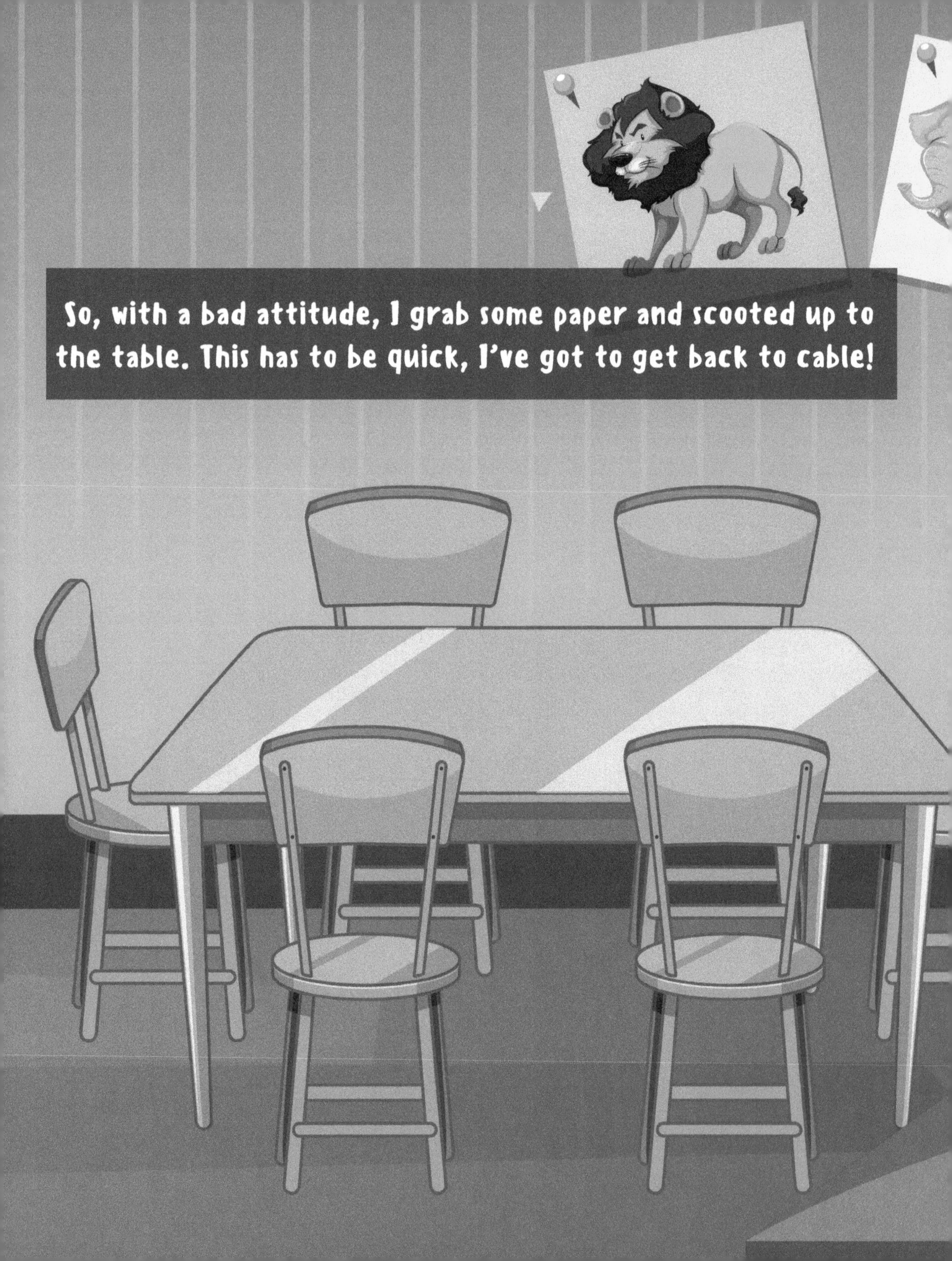

I spoke as I wrote, "Brown, Brown, it's not a clown. But I guess we all need brown around!"

"Um, I don't think so sir!", my mom said to me.
"Look the color brown up and tell me what you see!"

My dad cracked a smile and went back to snoring. I got up, grabbed the laptop, and started exploring.

The first thing that popped up was a lot of amazing brown things. Coats, horses, trees, and even ice cream. I kept scrolling until my screen was filled with brown.

Chocolate, squirrels, hairdos, and even coffee grounds. WOW! It was never-ending, it seemed like I was scrolling for hours. Keys, luggage, pretzels, footballs, and stacks of pennies that made dollars!

I got excited; I was ready to write. But then something caught my eye, I had to look again, I had to look twice! A brown ground, the color of earth's dirt. The mud and the soil that holds foundations of work!

How powerful is this brown that keeps buildings from leaning, that helps food to grow, and gives life's true meaning.

That was it, it was time to write. I've seen all I needed to see, to know the color brown is out of sight!

I held that brown crayon in one hand and wrote with the other. The words came easy and smooth as butter.

MY REPORT

PERIOD! It was done. I completed my assignment. Time for bed, the computer is dead, tomorrow I will be known as the class giant! Why? Because I won and conquered this homework.

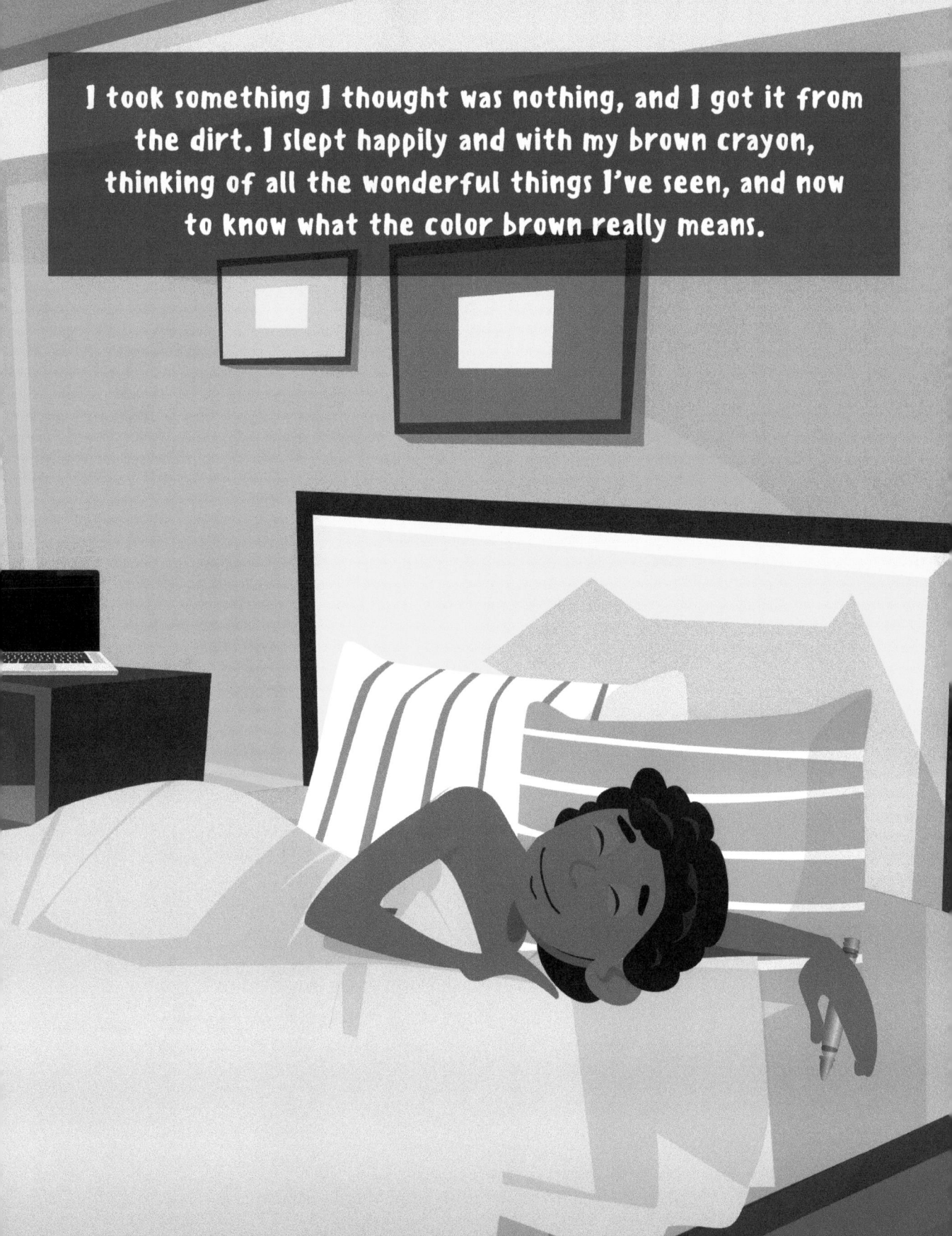

I took something I thought was nothing, and I got it from the dirt. I slept happily and with my brown crayon, thinking of all the wonderful things I've seen, and now to know what the color brown really means.

Well, the day is here, and Clarence is crying, but I don't care, my mind was flying.

I'm on a mission to tell the class what I found out,
I grabbed a muffin, an apple, and my bag off the couch!
I ran to the mirror for one last look.

WAIT! Who is that holding my books?!! It was proud, bold, with two feet for the ground.

It was smiling, it was winning, it was me, it was brown!

At that moment, everything had a different meaning, I realized the crayon I had been holding was me and my feelings. Ugly, lonely, and something nobody wanted to take home. Scared, dirty, and afraid to be alone.

I dropped my books, my apple fell and rolled like a ball, I touched the brown person in the mirror, and a tear began to fall. "I thought you knew", my dad said standing behind. "You are the best brown created in time!"

So, how did the poem turn out? I guess you want to ask.
Well, you've been reading it from the beginning, the one
I wrote for class.

Before I went to bed, I grabbed the brown crayon and went to the mirror.

"Thank you brown crayon, for helping me see things clearer!"

THE END

ABOUT THE AUTHOR

Michael G. Williams, born and raised in Garfield Heights, Ohio. Michael has over 22 years of experience as an Educator and Professional Development Leader in Social & Emotional Learning skills. He is also a college-educated Vocal Music Performer from Wright State University in Dayton, Ohio. Currently, Michael is a Dean of Engagement & Student Support for the Cleveland Metropolitan School District. He happily resides in Maple Heights, Ohio. He enjoys riding Rollercoasters, traveling, fishing, and spending time with his godchildren.

The Brown Crayon was written during the Covid-19 quarantine in 2020. In the midst of the George Floyd and Breonna Taylor protests, hate and racism gaining momentum, and our children, of every color, witnessing it all, Michael was lead by God to grab his laptop and begin to write. This is the first book Michael wrote! The Brown Crayon will show children that the color of their skin is not a crime. This book will show children how to love themselves and the beauty they actually possess! Enjoy and help spread the message of love!

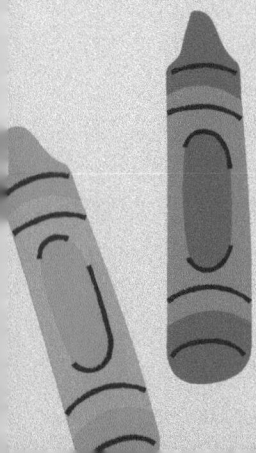

CPSIA information can be obtained
at www.ICGtesting.com
Printed in the USA
BVHW020219240821
615117BV00017B/901

9 781087 882994